D1237455

Based on the TV series *Rugrats*® created by Arlene Klasky, Gabor Csupo, and Paul Germain as seen on NICKELODEON®

SIMON SPOTLIGHT
An imprint of Simon & Schuster
Children's Publishing Division
1230 Avenue of the Americas
New York, NY 10020

GROLIER
B O O K S

This edition published by Grolier Books.
Grolier Books is a division of Grolier Enterprises, Inc.

ISBN 0-7172-6441-6

NICKELODEON®

Rugrats™

SURPRISE, ANGELICA!

By Becky Gold
Illustrated by Vince Giarrano

Simon Spotlight/Nickelodeon

"Get it, Spike!" Tommy called to his dog. He threw a ball in the air. Spike caught it. "Good boy!"

"Catching a ball is nothing," said Angelica. "Susie's new gerbils play *inside* balls."

"What are germ balls?" Tommy asked.

"Not germ balls, *gerbils*," Angelica replied. "They're a kind of rat who live in dark caves. And Susie has invited me over to see them."

"That sounds scary, Angelica!" exclaimed Chuckie.

Just then, Tommy's mom, Didi, called them in. "Susie's here," she said.

"Can we see Susie's gerbils, too?" Tommy asked Angelica.

"You babies stay here," Angelica warned. "Gerbils are very dangerous. They have sharp teeth that can chew through anything—high chairs . . . 'frigegators . . . everything!"

"Everything?" Chuckie gasped.

"That's right, Finster," Angelica said.

She wanted to be the first to see the gerbils.

"Hey, you guys are shivering like Jell-O," Susie said when she saw the babies. "What's the matter?"

"Susie, aren't you afraid to live with cave rats?" Chuckie asked.

"Yeah," said Tommy, 'specially ones with shark teeth?"

"You mean the gerbils? Why don't you come over to meet them?"

Tommy and Chuckie shook their heads. Susie stared at Angelica. She had a feeling she knew why they weren't coming over.

"So, Susie," said Angelica, "ready to go?"

"Tell you what," Susie said, "I'll go home first and prepare the gerbils for your visit. They don't like surprises. I'll come get you when they're ready."

"Oh, okay," Angelica said.

"Why she gots to repair them, Angelica?" asked Tommy.

"Yeah," Phil said. "Maybe they're broke."

"Maybe they gots too many germs!" Chuckie exclaimed.

"She said *prepare*, not repair, you dumb babies!" said Angelica.

When Susie got home, she told her brother Edwin how Angelica had scared Tommy, Chuckie, Phil, and Lil.

"Well, Suse," Edwin replied, "maybe Angelica just needs a taste of her own medicine. Come on, I'll help you."

After a while, Angelica started getting antsy. Those gerbils must be prepared enough, she thought. She went next door and rang the bell. Susie answered.

"I was just coming to get you," said Susie, huffing and puffing.

"Why are you breathing funny?" Angelica asked.

"I was running to get the gerbils more things to chew," Susie explained, "They're teething like crazy!"

"What's that?" asked Angelica. She pointed to the floor. It was covered with big, gray spots.

"Gerbil tracks," Susie said.

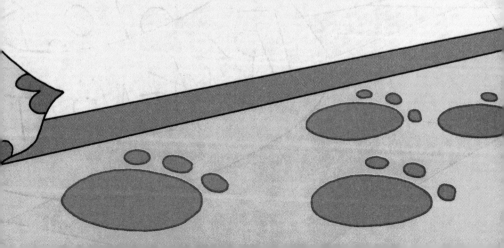

"Uh . . . is that their food?" asked
Angelica.

"Just a snack for later," Susie replied.
"This is Frankenrat's bowl . . . and this is
Igor's," she said, pointing. "And these are
boxes for them to chew on."

"Susie," said Angelica, "maybe the gerbils need to chew some more. Maybe they aren't ready to meet me yet. Maybe . . . we should go play outside!"

"No," Susie said. "They've been waiting for you! Follow me!" She led Angelica upstairs.

Suddenly, they heard a loud growl, followed by angry snarls. Angelica didn't know that Edwin was behind the door making the noises. She ran back down the stairs.

The doorbell rang again. It was Tommy, Chuckie, Phil, and Lil.

"Hi, gang!" Susie said.

"We were afraid," Tommy told her, "but a baby gots to be brave."

"So you're all ready to meet the gerbils?" Susie asked.

"YEAH!" cried Tommy, Phil, and Lil.

"N-n-no," said Chuckie.

"Hey, where's Angelica?" Tommy wondered.

"I don't know," said Susie. "She was here a minute ago."

"Who made the big poker dots?" asked Phil.

"Edwin did," Susie answered. "Come on upstairs."

"Oh, no," Chuckie mumbled. "I don't want to go up there!"

"Ooooooh!" exclaimed Lil.

"They don't look like rats," said Phil.

"And this doesn't look like a cave," added Lil.

"Gerbils aren't rats," said
Susie. "Angelica was just
scaring you."
   She gave them the gerbils
to hold.

"Gerbils are fuzzy," said Tommy.

"They don't bite," added Chuckie.

"And they don't growl," said Edwin. "But they *do* like to chew—on cardboard!"

Everyone took a turn at holding the gerbils.

"I need names for my gerbils," Susie told them. "Any ideas?"

"How about Frankenrat? Or Igor?" a voice said.

It was Angelica.

"You tricked me," she told Susie. "That was mean!"

"Well, you played a mean trick to keep the babies away!"

"Okay, okay," Edwin said. "Time to let bygones be bygones."

"Huh?" the babies said at once.

"Edwin's right," Susie said. She smiled and held out a gerbil. "Do you want to hold her?" she asked Angelica.

Angelica took the gerbil, which nuzzled her hand.

"Let's put them in their rockin' rollers," said Susie.

The babies chased the gerbils all over the floor.

Then, they watched them chew pieces of cardboard into tiny bits.

"Hey, this one runs fast," said Tommy.
"Can we call it Zoomer?"

"Sure, Tommy," Susie agreed. "And
because this one tickles, I'll call it Tickles!"

"Zoomer and Tickles, the bestest gerbils
in the world!" said Tommy.

People I Knowed

I'm Chuckie and, uh, I'm not so brave.
Here are some people I knowed my whole life:

This is Tommy.
the bravest baby
I ever knowed.

Here's Didi, Tommy's
mom. Now she's baby
Dil's mom, too.

This is baby Dil,
Tommy's brother,
he cries and
poops a lot. He
may be a baby, but
he's more trouble than a
carol full of monkeys!

This is Phil and Lil. Ummm . . .
uh, well, they like worms.

And um, here's Angelica. She's mean a lot. (But don't tell her I told you so!)

And this is Stu, Tommy and Dil's dad. He makes things. (Some are scary.)

Here's Tommy and Dil's Grandpa Lou. He has Paul's teeth (I've seen 'em in a glass!), and he tells good stories.

And this is Chaz, MY DAD! He's my favorite person.

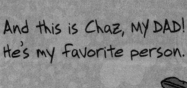

I Am Reptar, Hear Me Roar!

Now here's the one, the only,
Reptar wagon! It's the ultimate
in toddler transportation.
It's pretty amazing.

- It comfortably seats five babies.
- It has an emergency brake (red knob).
- It has automatic lifesaver capabilities.
- It has big bulging eyes – headlights to light the way on those evening jaunts.
- Fire shoots out of its mouth (optional) – good for those family camp-outs.
- It has voice activated recording devices.
- And its large teeth frighten off enemies.

Joke Break

If Tommy's cousin were a sandwich what kind would she be?

Peanut butter An-gelica.

Why did Tommy pull the plug in the bathtub?

He wanted to go for a drain ride.

What do fish use to calm their babies?

A bassifier.

Why are Rugrats like ink?

They're kept in a pen.

Why did Spike go to school?

He wanted to be the teacher's pet.

If Tommy's brother were a flower, what kind would he be?

A daffo-Dil.

If Chuckie were a cat, what kind would he be?

A scaredy-cat.

What does Dil throw best?

Tantrums.

Is Phil's twin big?

No, she's Lil.

If Phil and Lil were a piece of fruit, what kind would they be?

pear.

My Brother and ME

Things weren't so good in my house when Dil first came. He cried and cried and my mom and dad couldn't sleep. And then, he stealed my blankey.

Not having a baby brother means:

- Having Mom and Dad all to myself
- Mom and Dad can sleep all night—like babies!
- My blankey is my blankey.
- No head-bonking, nose-pulling, or Reptar-taking
- Not having to scare away wild monkeys who want to eat him.

But having a baby brother means:

- Being a big brother
- Having someone who looks up to me
- Getting a 'sponsitility
- Getting big baby hugs and big baby smiles
- Being a bigger fambly!

So I guess we'll keep him. Right, Dil?

It's Spike's Life

Spike became a hero when he tracked down the babies, chased some wild monkeys, and saved the babies from a mean and hungry wolf. But maybe he would rather have been:

- Chasing squirrels
- Sleeping in the sun
- Burying bones
- Sleeping on the couch

- Eating
- Chasing cars
- Chewing Stu's shoes
- Scratching his right ea

- Chasing birds
- Sniffing people
- Chasing his own tail
- Scratching his left ear
- Sleeping
- Getting a belly rub
- Barking at the dog next door